HEY, THAT'S MY MONSTER!

Written by
Amanda Noll

Illustrated by
Howard McWilliam

To my monsters, McKay, Brette, Casey, and Dylan. —AN
For Rebecca and my two favourite little monsters, Rufus and Miles. —HM

Free printable activity pages available on our website.
Editor: Shari Dash Greenspan
Graphic Design: The Virtual Paintbrush
This book was typeset in Kingston, a font designed by Howard McWilliam.
The illustrations were drawn with pencil on paper, and colored with digital paint.
Distributed by IPG • www.ipgbook.com
Flashlight Press • 527 Empire Blvd. • Brooklyn, NY 11225 • www.FlashlightPress.com

Flash Light PRESS

Tonight, when I looked under the bed for my monster, I found this note instead.

So long, kid.
Gotta go.
Someone needs me
more than you do.

—Gabe

What?! Gabe was MY monster!
Nobody needed him more than me!

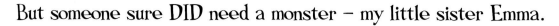

But someone sure DID need a monster – my little sister Emma.

Now that Emma slept in a toddler bed, she liked to...

...climb out,

roam the house,

and play noisy games at night.

I knew a monster would keep her in bed so she could fall asleep.

But not MY monster!
I *had* to get Gabe back.

I tiptoed across the hall to Emma's room.

She wasn't even there.

But Gabe was!
I gulped, zoomed across
the carpet, and leaped
onto Emma's bed before
Gabe could grab my toes.

"Gabe," I whispered.
"Please go back to our room.
I'll get Emma to sleep."

"You?!" he snorted.
"You're gonna
get her to sleep?
Ha! That's a good one!
But you know what?
I like you, kid, so I'll give you
three chances. If she's not
asleep, I'll be back!"

And Gabe
was gone.

Just then Emma toddled into the room.
She clearly needed a monster.

Maybe she didn't know how to get one.

But *I* did.

"Hey, Emma," I said.
"Let's play. Can you
knock on the floor?"

Emma knocked –
with a dinosaur.

It worked.
I heard some creaking
under Emma's bed.
Then something
sniffled.
It squelched
and dripped.

So far so good, I thought.
This monster sounds
scary enough for Emma.

But Emma kept on playing.

A slime-covered monster slid out.
It oozed toward Emma.

"Icky!" she laughed, wiping
one of the monster's noses.
"Icky! Wipe!"

Emma wasn't scared at all!

"Excuse me," I said to the mucus monster. "I didn't catch your name."

"By dabe is Agatha," she said through stuffed noses. "Tibe for bed, Ebba."

Emma giggled and wiped some more.

I knew this wouldn't work. "Thanks, Agatha. Nice try. But I think we need a monster with claws."

Agatha snuffled, and then she was gone.

"Emma," I coaxed again,
"knock, knock."

She knocked on the floor –
with a teapot this time –
and I heard more creaking.

Then a slippery tail
slithered out from
under the bed.

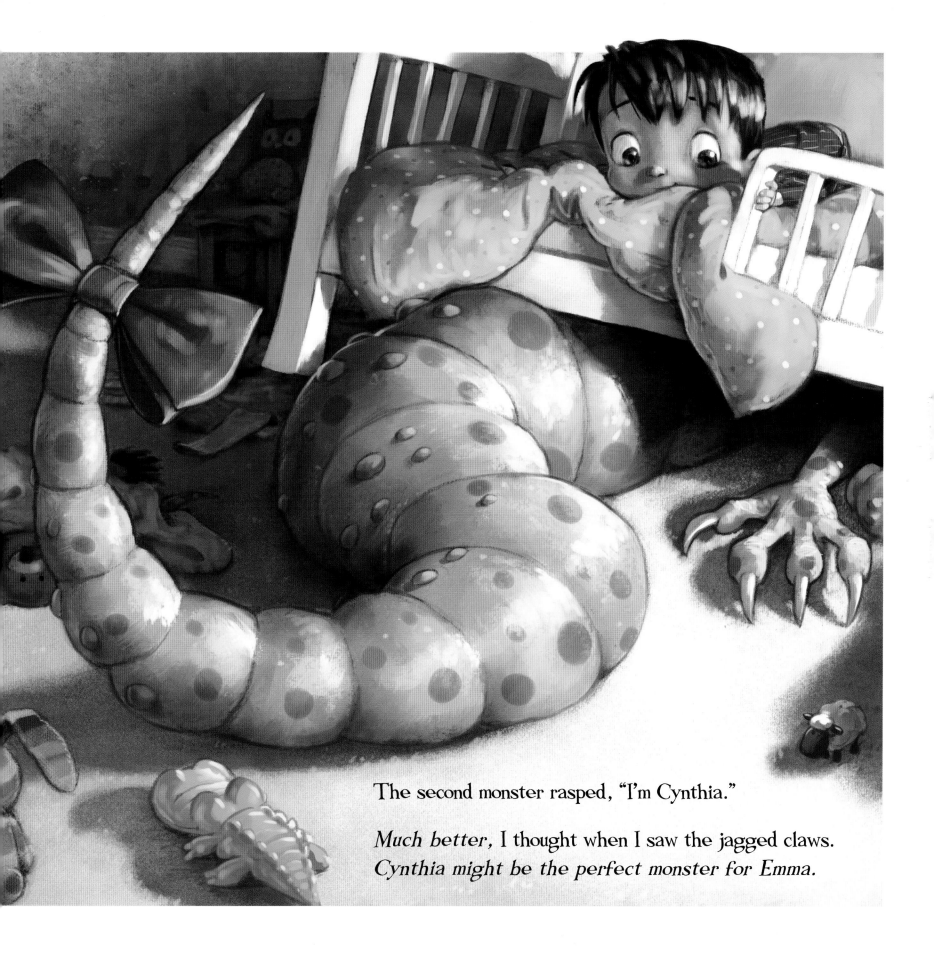

The second monster rasped, "I'm Cynthia."

Much better, I thought when I saw the jagged claws.
Cynthia might be the perfect monster for Emma.

But Emma blinked and said, "Pretty!"

Then she decorated Cynthia's tail
with bracelets.

"Ugh," Cynthia snarled. "I'm not here to play dress up! I'm here to scare you into bed!" Cynthia rattled loudly, but Emma danced to the beat.

"I'm sorry, Cynthia," I said. "This isn't going to work."

"Well, I never!" she sniffed, and then she was gone.

"Cymfia, come back!" Emma demanded, stomping on the floor.

Excellent, I thought. *Maybe **that** would summon the perfect monster for Emma.*

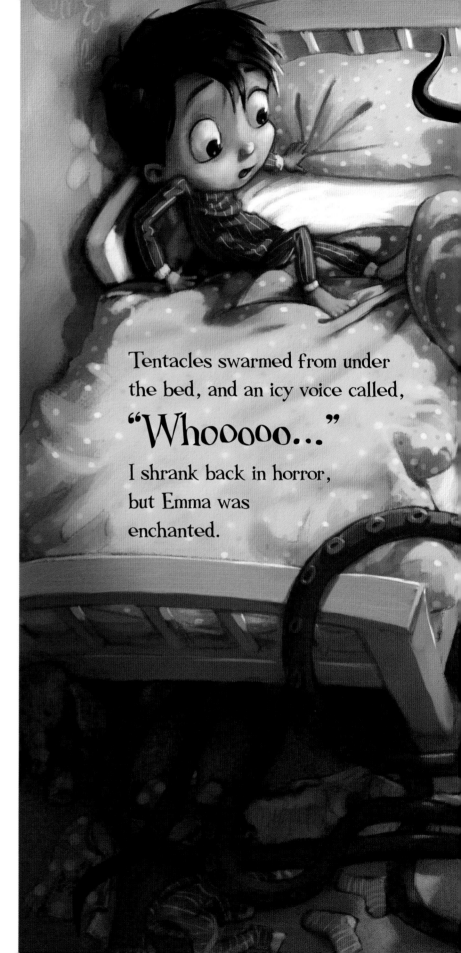

Tentacles swarmed from under the bed, and an icy voice called,

"Whooooo..."

I shrank back in horror, but Emma was enchanted.

"Whoooo's out of bed?" the monster continued. "Come to Vla-a-adimir...."

Emma high-fived one of the tentacles, and the third monster emerged.

I already had doubts about this one, but he was my last chance.
"Vladimir," I asked, "can you get Emma to sleep?"

"Yes-s-s-s," he hissed, reaching for Emma. "I can GET her!"

Emma giggled and hopped over the tentacles like jump ropes.

"Oh, no!" I blurted. "She's not supposed to be having fun! This'll never work!"

Vlad's tentacles drooped, he slunk under the bed, and he was gone.

"Sorry, Vlad…" I called.

Boy, was I sorry. I was about to lose Gabe – forever.

Now Emma
was coloring.
And singing.
"Blabamir, bla, bla,
Cymfia, ya, ya,
Agafa, fa, fa...."

Gabe must have heard her,
because he was back.
"That's it, kid," he grunted.
"You had your three tries.
Now it's MY turn."

Gabe's green ooze sizzled across
the floor as he growled,

"Put. The crayon. Down."

Emma peered at my hulking,
sharp-clawed monster
and said,
"Fuzzy."

"Hey, Gabe!" I cheered.
"Emma isn't afraid of you!"

"*WHAT?!!*" Gabe burst out from under the bed and loomed over Emma. Steam spurted from his ears.

"Get.
Into.
Bed!"

Gabe thundered.

Emma hopped up. But she kept singing, "Fuzzy, fuzzy monster."

"Gabe," I said, "Emma's not scared enough to fall asleep. Please, let's go back to our room."

"No can do, kid," Gabe growled. "I may not be the perfect monster for Emma, but I'm the best so far. At least she's in bed now. I gotta stay here. You're on your own."

I knew Emma needed Gabe, but he was MY monster. How was I ever going to get to sleep without him?

Just then, we heard a tiny noise.

hic.
hic.
hic.

Emma froze. Gabe and I peered
under the bed.

"Stella, what are *you* doing here?" Gabe asked.

"Hi, Gabe," Stella said, tugging on her tutu. "You forgot –hic– your snack. Mama thought –hic– you'd be hungry, so she –hic– sent this."

Who knew? Gabe had a little sister too!

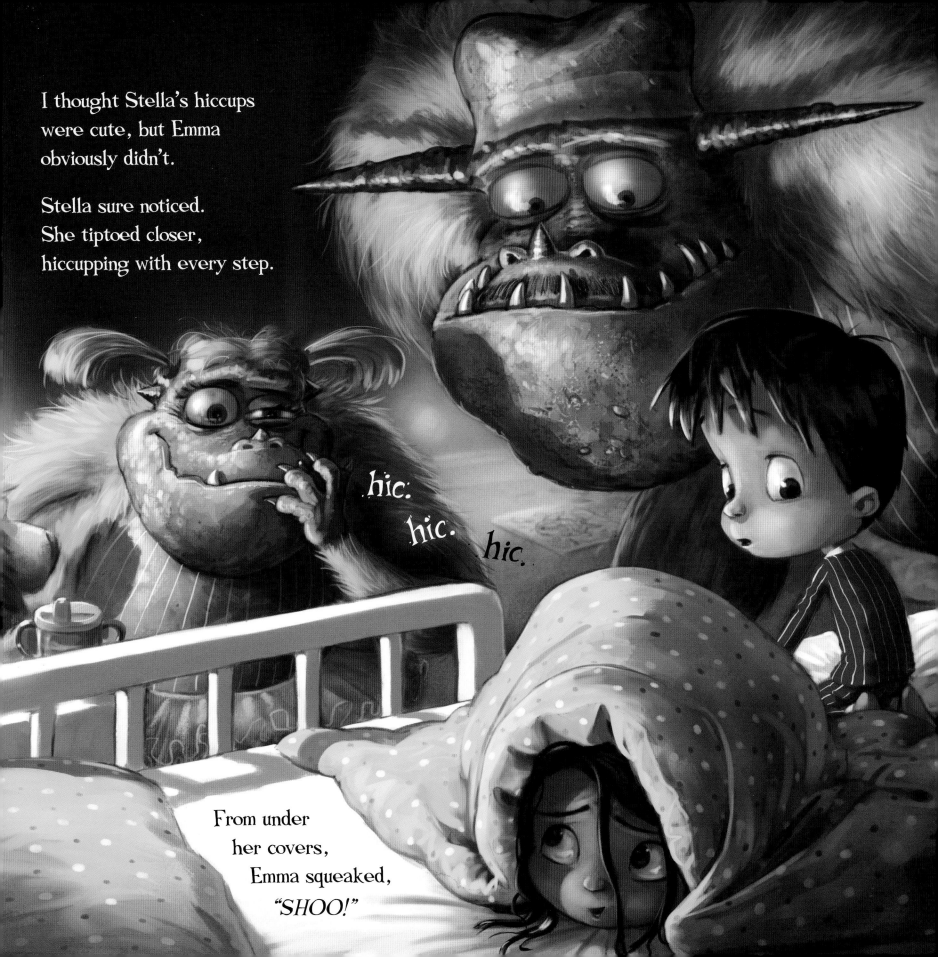

I thought Stella's hiccups were cute, but Emma obviously didn't.

Stella sure noticed. She tiptoed closer, hiccupping with every step.

hic.
hic.
hic.

From under her covers, Emma squeaked, *"SHOO!"*

"Shoo?" Stella repeated. "Oh! Shoe! That's where toes go. I *loooove* toes." Stella crept toward Emma's feet.

Emma squealed,
   scrunched in her feet,
   and giggled,
   "No toes,
no toes!"

Gabe laughed. "Stella, it looks like you're the perfect monster for Emma. Now, if you don't mind, *you* can get her to sleep while *I* get back to what *I* do best."

Stella nodded. *"Hic!"*

I sighed with relief and switched off Emma's lamp.

Then I ran to my room, leaped into bed, and scrunched in my feet so Gabe couldn't get them.

I shivered happily.

Emma had Stella.
I had Gabe.
Everything was back to normal.

I shivered again.

We'd all be asleep in no time.